PITTMAN

Jared R. Teer

Strategic Book Publishing and Rights Co.

Strategic Book Publishing and Rights Co., LLC
USA | Singapore
www.sbpra.net

For information about special discounts for bulk purchases, please contact Strategic Book Publishing and Rights Co., LLC. Special Sales, at bookorder@sbpra.net.

ISBN: 978-1-68235-329-5

There wasn't much to look at in the old neighborhood—trees, brick walls, dilapidated buildings, and disillusioned denizens.

Detective Celeste Jacquet knew the ward inside and out, not just from her days as a patrol officer on these streets, but she was born and raised here.

She was one of the fortunate ones. Once going down the same path of destruction upon which so many from this community found themselves, Coach's boxing gym provided the diversion she needed to right her course. Coach was a sly one. When Celeste was a teenager, Coach got her to come to his gym with promises of taking her street-fighting skills to the next level. What ultimately developed was a work ethic and discipline that made her forever grateful.

Coach was instrumental in giving many youths from the area hope for a better tomorrow and the focus to pursue it. Coach's Bayou Boxing was a staple in the community, and Detective Jacquet knew if anyone had some information, it would be him.

A veteran and retiree from the Army Special Forces, Coach came from a family with deep roots in New Orleans going back for generations of free people of color. He inherited a historic, two-story house and converted the first floor into a gym. Maintaining an old house like that might not be worth it to some, seeing that it was in a depressed area of the city, but Coach saw it as an opportunity to give back to the community. He took up boxing in the military and wanted to open a boxing gym in the hood, and with a little ingenuity, the old house afforded him the opportunity.

There was no training on Sundays, so Celeste knew he would be available to talk. As she pulled up in front of Coach's, she saw that things had changed. The old house looked to have had some upgrades recently—a new fence and new paint. She made it up the long walkway and rang the bell.

"Here I come!" Coach said from inside. "CJ!" he exclaimed as he greeted her with a hug. Coach was a tall, thick man, not the lean, fighting machine of his youth, but in impressive shape for someone sixty-five years of age. "It's been a while. It's good to see you, CJ."

"You too, Coach."

"Come in!"

Detective Jacquet, or CJ, as Coach called her, noticed that there had been some improvements to the gym as well. Coach took out the walls that could be removed to open up space and reinforced the ceiling to support the heavy bags. The ceiling was high enough to accommodate a standard ring without the fighters needing to bend down to spar.

"Coach, the place looks great! You got the nice punching bags now! Is that a new ring?"

"Yeah, donations have been pouring in lately. For Remy, you know," Coach said in a somber tone.

Detective Jacquet took on a serious demeanor. "About that, Coach, I have some news that I wanted to tell you in person. They're all dead. All of the people suspected in Remy's disappearance were killed in a massacre at the Armand plantation."

Coach simply closed his eyes while slowly nodding his head.

Detective Jacquet continued. "We still don't have any leads on Remy's whereabouts, and getting any now will definitely be more difficult with all the suspects dead. I've never seen anything like it. The crime scene was like a bloodbath out of a horror movie. Nearly two dozen armed men were all apparently bludgeoned to death and dismembered. Armed gunmen, professional bodyguards, all killed, and not a single gunshot wound in any of their bodies."

"You don't say. That's all very odd. I appreciate you for keeping me informed, CJ."

"Yeah, odd is one way to describe it. I can think of some more expletive-laden descriptions too. Anyway, I just wanted you to know. It's all so crazy. Maybe I thought you could shed some light on the situation."

"Celeste, I look at you like a daughter. All of the youngsters who come through here are special, but you were always different. I've always been proud of what you've become. You went to college, joined the force, became a detective. But don't forget where you come from—this is New Orleans. Everything in this world ain't meant for people to understand.

"Remy was like a son to me after I adopted him when his parents died. He didn't have anybody else. He was on his way to the top! With that victory over Tarpin, he was in line to get a title shot. Twenty-one years old and a title shot! A young black man with unlimited potential! All his hard work was paying off."

"That's why I'm here, Coach. In a way, justice was served. But can there ever be closure with all these mysterious

7

circumstances? We have no idea what happened there, plus Remy missing and presumed to be ..."

"It sounds like they got what they deserved. Like I told you before, the day of the fight with Tarpin, two of Adrien Armand's goons approached Remy and tried to get him to throw the fight. They had a motive, so that's it—they did it. Remy and Adrien's little brother have been rivals since PAL boxing. The sons of bitches knew that a loss for Remy would up that piece of crap Antoine's stock in the title hunt. Antoine "The Alligator" Armand. Little twerp . . . excuse me for that, CJ. Antoine was never really a bad kid. It was his brother Adrien who was the problem. Remy always had Antoine's number though, being a five-foot-eleven-inch middleweight who was good in all aspects, of course he would win.

"It just seems like they got what they deserved. They gave Remy an ultimatum—lose the fight or die. Yeah, right. They obviously didn't know Remy. He told me what happened that evening while I was wrapping his hands for the fight. I could see the bruising on his knuckles from what he did to them. I called him a dummy for hurting his hands before a big fight. It didn't matter though. You saw it. First-round KO!

"The day after the fight, as Remy was known to do, he went to his parents' graves to pay his respects. You know Remy, always training. What's a ten-mile jog to the cemetery and back? Just walking the dog, right?"

"And that's when he disappeared," CJ cut in. "We know foul play was involved but couldn't tie it to Armand. Investigators found Remy's blood at the cemetery. There was the shallow grave that had been smoothed over. Remy's blood was in the grave, but there was no body. They found Remy's dog buried there, but not Remy."

"How do you explain that?" Coach asked.

"Well, he didn't crawl out of the grave and walk away. Apparently, the people who buried him decided they should get rid of the body," CJ responded.

"You sure about that?"

"Well, let me think, Coach . . . yes, I'm sure! They figured no body, so no evidence."

"No, I mean the first thing you said. You sure he didn't crawl out of the grave and walk away?"

"Like a zombie, Coach? Come on now."

"Humor me, CJ. Maybe I'm crazy. Maybe all of this finally pushed me over the edge, and I lost it. What they did to Remy was unforgivable. They killed him on the grounds of his parents' graves. But you can't kill justice. You can't bury it. Sometimes blood cries so loud from the grave that the earth can't keep it buried.

"What if I told you Remy came home the day they killed him?"

* * *

It was early Sunday morning after the big fight, and as was his tradition, Remy planned to go tell his parents how he'd done. You wouldn't catch many fighters who were willing to exercise the day after a fight, but Remy saw things differently. Training wasn't a burden to him but a part of who he was. Coach and boxing were there for him at his lowest point, and committing himself to the rigors was his way of giving back.

His blue pit bull Champ didn't share Remy's enthusiasm, but after they got going, Champ was a good jogging companion. Remy stayed in the basement under the gym at Coach's place. Not a gloomy basement that some might imagine in an old house like that, it was fitted with modern upgrades and was spacious, more like a studio apartment than a Victorian cellar.

He geared up and latched Champ to a long chain leash and took off, about five miles there and five back. *Light work.* Remy figured he'd be back before Coach woke up to make coffee.

He arrived at the cemetery as the sunrise illuminated the grounds with streaks of light shining through the tall trees like the spotlights that shined on him the previous night. He made his way through the grounds, slowing as he approached his parents' plot. The chirping birds must have been getting to Champ as he emitted a low growl. "Shhh, calm down, boy."

He looked solemnly at the headstone: *BELOVED PARENTS AND FRIENDS—REGIS & HELENA PITTMAN.*

"Hey, Ma. Hey, Dad. Looks like it's gonna be a nice day today. Did y'all see me last night? It was a great performance. Your baby boy is now the number-one-ranked professional middleweight in the world! It's looking like I get a shot at the title next! I'm just thankful. Thank you for looking over me. I know I gotta stay humble."

Champ started growling, and Remy turned to see at what. Coming from behind some trees were the two goons who had tried to intimidate him into throwing the fight. One had a wide bandage over his nose, and the other was wearing shades to cover his black eyes.

"You two didn't get enough last night, huh? Show some respect. I don't want any trouble here," Remy warned.

The one with the broken nose spoke. "You got trouble, asshole. Didn't we warn you what would happen if it didn't go down how we told you? But hey, at least you can get to see your parents sooner rather than later."

The goon started to reach into his jacket. Remy let Champ go, and the dog burst forward, biting into the man's inner thigh and thrashing. The other goon backed away and pulled a pistol. He put two rounds into Champ. Remy ran toward him as the goon turned the gun to take aim. Moving forward, Remy attempted to lean out of the line of fire while closing in. Two rounds impacted his upper chest, spinning him to the ground.

"You think you can dodge bullets, tough guy?" He kicked Remy in the gut, flipping him over onto his back. Pointing the gun down at Remy's chest, he said, "You win some, and you lose some." Then he emptied the magazine.

* * *

In the darkness he became aware. *Cold. Tight. Help!* He didn't know up from down. As he exerted himself, the weight upon him gave way. Light and air greeted him as he crawled from the dirt. It was nighttime. Memories of what happened came in relentless waves. *They shot me!* He checked where he had been shot—no wounds. He remembered Champ. He turned toward the upheaved dirt of the shallow grave and frantically dug. *Champ . . . no.* He laid Champ in the grave and petted him gently before covering him over and smoothing the dirt.

As he kneeled there, anger welled inside. His dark eyes became a fiery amber. It felt like fire was running through his veins as he shook with rage. He let out a prolonged cry that grew more guttural and blaring as it continued. He snarled, baring his gnashing teeth and shaking. His canine teeth elongated. There came crackling sounds from within his body as his muscles tensed, the veins rising and throbbing. His brow furrowed and his nose flared as his facial bones elongated into a wide muzzle. His bones and muscles began to grow and swell, his feet burst from his sneakers, and his limbs stretched his sweats to tatters.

His terrible transformation complete, the hulking vision from a nightmare, now afraid and confused, turned to where it felt safe—home.

* * *

Coach was startled from his sleep by a familiar knock at the door. *Remy! It's the middle of the night! What the hell, boy! Where have you been?*

Coach ran down the steps and opened the door.

The thing towering before him had the large, broad head of a giant American pit bull terrier, with short, glossy, bluish-gray fur. It stood about six feet eight on padded toes, with wide shoulders and a frame packed with ripped muscles that were defined through the fur. Draped over its shoulders were the remnants of a tattered black sweatshirt, shredded black shorts barely clung to its groin, and a thick, pointy tail poked out at the rear.

Horror overtook Coach, and he fell backward, unconscious.

"Coach, Coach! Wake up! You passed out!" Remy said, his voice now freakishly deep and guttural.

"Remy?" Coach opened his eyes and gazed upon the monstrosity looking at him as it kneeled beside his bed. Coach closed his eyes in fear. "Lord Jesus, I'm sorry! I repent! I know I've done a lot of bad things, but I repent, Lord! Have mercy on me!"

"Coach! Coach! It's me! It's Remy!"

"You don't sound like Remy, and you damn sure don't look like him!"

"Coach, you're supposed to be the calm one, remember? I'm the one you always told to relax."

His eyes still closed, Coach said, "Remy, what the hell is going on? Why do you look like that? Like a damn bear!"

"Coach, it's me. Just keep your eyes closed if that helps. All I know is this . . ."

Remy recounted the events to Coach, from his jog to visit his parents' graves, to the transformation.

"I just wanted to come home," Remy continued. Getting the story out had a calming effect on Remy, and a cooling sensation came over his body. It felt like a continuous exhalation as the fur began to retract and his muscles started to shrink.

"Coach! Something is happening to me!" Remy said in a cracking voice.

Coach noticed the change in Remy's voice and opened his eyes to observe him changing back into his normal self.

"Coach . . . *help me.*"

* * *

On a plantation estate on the banks of the Mississippi River, crime boss Adrien Armand observed his little brother Gator's training session, pleased in knowing that he was responsible for eliminating his sibling's biggest rival. Not one who desired to train in front of admiring fans, the only spectators here were his trainers, the numerous bodyguards under his brother's employment, the animal attendants—and the alligators.

The Armand family was one of the richest and most powerful crime families in the world, having roots in New Orleans dating back to antebellum. The patriarch of the family was a French nobleman who fled to America during the French Revolution. Publicly, the Armands were believed to have gained their wealth from growing sugar cane, but in reality, they were disciples of black magic, combining Western European occultism with the voodoo practices of the slaves under their subjugation. Through the appeasement of demons by blood sacrifices, the Armands were able to amass great wealth and maintain a veneer of good repute.

Adrien's wife, Veronique, was exceptionally adept in the dark practices, being known in the inner circles as a voodoo queen. An ethnic Creole, it was Veronique's dark magic that empowered and sustained the current generation of the Armand dynasty.

With wealth exceeded only by his profligate tendencies, Adrien spared no expense when it came to shamelessly promoting his brother's boxing career, going as far as to adorn his training facility with live alligator tanks and enclosures, dubbing it the Alligator Pen. The immense training facility looked more like a herpetarium than a boxing gym. A large boxing ring occupied a platform in the center of the facility, surrounded by a circular expanse that diverged into trails that led to the various training areas—heavy bags, weight equipment, and speed bags. Interspersed throughout the winding trails were live alligator exhibits behind reinforced glass, complete with ponds and flora. An alligator tank befitting an exhibit at a zoo ran the length of the western wall, with pictures of Antoine "The Alligator" Armand, Gator as he was called, in action spread above it.

Gator was wrapping up a training session on the speed bag. Though he was short for the middleweight division at five feet seven inches, his aggressive style, constant pressure, and knockout power made Gator a crowd-pleaser and a must-watch fighter in the division. He had an undefeated record and was in the title picture, as was Remy.

Remy and Gator had fought a couple times in the amateurs, Remy getting the better of him on both occasions due to his ring generalship. With his win over the former champion Tarpin, Remy was in line to get the next shot at the current champ and all the fanfare that came with it.

That didn't sit well with Adrien. He'd be damned if someone other than his brother brought the pro title back to New Orleans.

"Time!" shouted the trainer, and Gator threw a final swing to the speed bag.

Adrien approached his brother with exuberance, with Veronique at his side. "My man! The champ is *right here*! You're going straight to the top, baby bro! Nobody's even close to this guy!"

15

"Yeah? We'll never know now," Gator replied dejectedly.

"What? You giving me crap for clearing the path for you? Screw that ghetto trash. If it wasn't us, somebody woulda smoked his ass over some ghetto drama, right? Get outa here, bro. You hear this guy, baby?"

"Your brother only has the family's . . . *your*, best interests in mind, Antoine," Veronique said. "These days, such fidelity is a rarity. You should appreciate what your brother does for you."

Looking at Veronique sternly, Gator responded, "I'm a fighter. Win or lose, I'm in it for the challenge." He then turned to his brother. "You never understood that."

"Naw, baby bro, *YOU* never understood that this ain't a damn game. We play to win! Screw some feelings! That's why you were never cut out for this gangster life. Keep training to whoop ass before I whoop your ass. Get outa here. Love you."

"Yeah, love you too."

At that moment, Adrien received a phone call from one of his plants in the NOPD, and he walked away to take the call.

Veronique addressed Gator. "Do try to understand, Antoine. Your brother only has your best interests in mind."

"I'm not stupid, V. I know the reasons for the family's power. That's one of the things that drove me to be a fighter. I wanted to feel like I earned anything I achieved."

Veronique laughed. "What a silly sentiment. Fools toil by the sweat of their brows day after day and achieve little of any significance. Your ancestor knew this, which is why he left France during the delusional advocation of social equality at the time. In this world, it is the birthright of the strong to impose their will on those born of lesser stock. You would do well to remember this truth."

"What the . . . hell!" Adrien blurted to the informant. "Okay. Let me know the second you hear anything." Adrien, highly perturbed, made his way back over to Antoine and Veronique. "That was my guy in the NOPD. Apparently, Remy's body wasn't found at the cemetery. Can anyone explain to me how the hell that is possible? Anyone?"

The two goons who carried out the hit looked at each other perplexed.

"You," he said to the one with the blackened eyes. "You told me it was handled. You said you put eight rounds in his chest and buried his ass with the damn dog. Am I missing something?"

"Nu . . . no, boss, that's what happened. I swear to God," he replied nervously.

"My guy in the NOPD is telling me that the only body found was the damn dog. You telling me the body evaporated like Obi-Wan Palpatine or some crap? Is that what you're telling me?"

"No, boss . . . no! He was there with me. Remy is dead!" he said, indicating his partner.

"It's true, boss," said the one with the broken nose.

"Gator, whoop these dummies' asses," Adrien said to his brother.

Gator shrugged his shoulders and unhesitatingly dropped the one with the blackened eyes with a straight to the jaw and a hook to the gut.

The other held his hands in front of him, pleading, but Gator crouched with a straight to the gut under his outstretched arms, followed by an uppercut to the chin.

The two goons writhed in pain on the floor.

"That's what I'm talking about, baby bro," Adrien cheered. "Now finish them off."

Gator looked at his brother questioningly.

"See, baby," Adrien said to his wife, "I told you he was never cut out for this gangster life."

The anger from a lifetime of trying to show his big brother how strong he was and never seeming to do enough boiled over, and Gator went numb. He reached his hand out to help the one with the blackened eyes get up. As he reached up for Gator's hand, Gator snatched him by the wrist and lifted him onto his shoulders in a fireman's carry. Gator then briskly walked to one of the alligator pens and launched the goon into it.

Gator watched stoically as he was torn to pieces.

"Holy crap, bro!" Adrien exclaimed, overcome with glee. "Did you see that, baby? My baby bro's first kill, and it's a masterpiece!"

Gator looked over at the goon with the broken nose and said, "Time for the encore."

* * *

Remy was accustomed to getting up early, so the sleepless night occupied with relentless thoughts of his predicament was reconciled as motivation to get up and train. Train hard and fight easy was his motto, and he believed that getting up early to run gave him an edge over the competition.

Remy started the day with his regular five-mile run, but there was nothing regular about this morning. It was like being on a motorcycle, the wind in his face and the effortless drive of his legs felt like something out of a dream. He did his typical roadwork around the community and back home, but he wasn't winded in the slightest, and it only took five minutes. The sun wasn't up, so he figured he'd take another run, and another, and another.

This time when he got back home, Coach was waiting on the porch with his morning coffee. It was the crack of dawn and the sky was a fiery hue.

"How was your run?" Coach asked.

"It's hard to put into words," Remy replied. "It was like being in a car, with how fast everything was passing by. I did at least ten goes of my usual five miles, and I'm not even tired!"

"Remy, you asked me to help you. I'd be a liar if I said I had all the answers. I do know one thing though, and that's how to train. Let's figure this out together."

Under Coach's keen eye, Remy started the session with some rope skipping. He started casually, but almost immediately went into double-unders, then triple-unders, and quadruple-unders. Decuple-unders seemed to be the happy medium, so he did those for the remainder of the three rounds of warmup.

Coach, clearly awestruck, attempted to maintain an air of command over the training session and took charge.

"Time. Good work. Now glove up. Mitt rounds."

After years of training together, their pad work was synchronized to the point where Remy could close his eyes and not miss a beat.

"You ready?" Coach asked. Remy nodded.

Coach jabbed at Remy's head with the mitt. "Where ya at? Whatcha gonna do? Focus." Coach held the mitt upright. "Jab!"

Remy threw a jab to the mitt.

"Aaaaahhhhh!" Coach yelled in pain. He staggered around, clutching his shoulder in agony.

"Coach! What's wrong?"

"It's okay! I'm okay! It's just a little dislocated, that's all. It's happened before. Give me a minute."

It had never happened before. After agonizing for a few minutes, Coach popped his shoulder back into place and was ready to go.

"Okay! I think that's enough pad work for now. Let's try the heavy bag. Start with some light jabs, then rip some hooks to the body."

Remy nodded, and the round timer signaled.

Remy simply touched the bag with his jab a couple times and then ripped a right hook to the body that shot the stuffing out of the other side of the leather bag and tore it from the chain. He looked over at Coach with a dejected look on his face.

"Okay!" Coach said enthusiastically. "Good session! Let's wrap it up with something safe: shadowboxing."

* * *

In an armory across town, six professional killers were gearing up for a night on the job. The leader of the crew was on the phone, receiving final instructions from Adrien Armand.

"I don't want any screw-ups this time. Kill whoever is there and burn the place down," Adrien instructed.

"Got it, boss," the leader of the hit men replied, and the call ended. "Okay, lock and load, boys."

One of the assassins questioned, "Why is the boss sending our team to handle this light work? It's just two guys."

"The old man was supposed to be a badass back in the day," the leader responded. "The boss really wants these guys dead. Apparently, they have some history with the boss's brother. I'm not worried about the boxer. If he's even still alive, he won't be in any shape to put up a fight. The boss just wants confirmation. Let's get it done."

* * *

Remy and Coach were in the kitchen discussing the training session over dinner. Coach always made a lot, never knowing if someone might pop over, which was fortunate because Remy seemed insatiable. Remy was on his fourth heaping bowl of gumbo.

"Remy, you know my philosophy: there are no problems, there are only solutions. Your power is incredible. If you hit somebody, you're gonna kill 'em. Let's just be honest. And your speed is like nothing I've ever seen.

"This is all so crazy, but we have to figure it out. I don't want you to get a big head. You gotta be humble in this life. You gotta keep learning. You gotta be willing and receptive. These gifts you have are things people only dream of. You can't run with that though and think you don't have to put in any work. The work we put in is a way to show appreciation for what we have.

"That being said, there's always things to improve and work on. The way to get better is to work on the things that don't come easy, right? Well, you got the speed, and you got the strength. What you're lacking is control. When you can control your abilities, then you're talkin' about somethin'. So, you haven't had any more transformations?"

Remy shook his head no. "Not since that night."

"Strange," said Coach. "Even so, obviously, you're different. Maybe the change was a one-time thing. Maybe something triggers it. I don't—"

Remy cut him off. "Coach, we got company."

"What? How do you know?" Coach asked, bewildered.

"I heard them pull up front," Remy replied.

"Okay, I'll handle it. Go downstairs. I know you don't like hiding, but until we figure things out, this is how it has to be."

Remy sulked off to his room.

Out front, a dark SUV had parked. The six hit men exited the vehicle and made their way to the house.

The doorbell rang. "Here I come," Coach yelled as he ran to the door and opened it.

"Hey, Coach, can we come in?" asked the leader before kicking in the door and walking in.

"What the hell is this?" Coach demanded.

"Coach, we just want to see if Remy is home. Have you seen him lately?"

"Did Armand send you? How about you ask your boss where Remy's at. He's the one who was responsible for his disappearance."

"Naw, that's where you're wrong," the lead goon replied. "We know exactly where that piece of crap was buried. What we don't know is who dug him up. We figured you could fill us in on that part."

"Go to hell."

"Beat his ass," the leader commanded, and the five goons circled Coach.

The first to approach was floored by a right cross. The next ate an uppercut but managed to wrap his arms around Coach's waist in a bear hug. The rest of the goons took advantage of this and beat Coach to the floor, where they stomped and kicked him savagely.

"That's good," said the lead goon, and the rest backed away.

Coach was a battered mess. Regardless, he defiantly said, "I train kids who hit harder than you losers."

The lead goon chuckled. "You make a better punching bag than a boxing coach. Last chance, old man. Where . . . is . . . Remy?"

"Piss off."

"Welp, I tried," he said as he reached inside his jacket and pulled out a revolver. He pointed it down at Coach and cocked the hammer.

At that moment, the hulking, blue-gray monstrosity exploded from the floor between the leader and Coach. As it stalked toward the goon, the goon unloaded six rounds into the beast to no avail. The beast then shifted forward with a lead hook that knocked his head clean off, sending it hurtling into the wall. His body slumped to the floor in a heap.

The henchmen stared aghast at their fallen leader and drew their guns.

The next two to fall were standing next to each other. They fired at the spot where the beast had been, registering too late that he had sidestepped, darted forward, and was upon them. It threw a right straight into the chest of the closest one that impacted with a terrible crunch and knocked him into his partner with such force that it sent them both crashing onto the floor. The one who was punched in the chest lay gurgling and convulsing on top of his partner, his ribcage and spine shattered; the man beneath him was motionless, his skull crushed from the impact of his head hitting the floor.

The fourth to fall got a couple shots off toward the back of its head as it was looking down at the previous two casualties. The angered beast pivoted around to face him. He let off more shots, but they only seemed to further enrage the beast. The beast dashed forward and was next to him before he realized it. It snatched his pistol away, and with the same hand, it backfisted him with such force that he flipped backward off the ground, his head dangling back grotesquely on a broken neck.

The next one to fall attempted to turn and run, but the beast punched him in the back with such force that it burst his entrails out of his anterior; his lifeless body skidded to a stop just before the last of his associates. At the sight of his mangled teammates, the last of them decided that he would take his chances with becoming alligator bait and made a retreat out the front door.

The beast knelt beside Coach, placing a hand on his shoulder.

"Looking good, kid. Nice footwork."

"Coach, you're hurt bad," it said somberly in its guttural voice.

"Be quiet. I've taken a few ass whoopins in my day. This ain't the worst or the last."

The beast smiled. "They're going to pay for what they've done."

"Remy, listen to me. I think I know why you've been given these powers. You're a curse. Help me up." Remy helped him to his feet.

"I'm cursed, Coach?"

"No! You *are* a curse, a punishment upon people like these. How many times do evil people get away with the things they do? They didn't with you. I'm proud of you, son."

With those words from Coach, Remy knew what he had to do. The Armands had to be stopped, and he'd come back from the grave—*to send them to theirs.*

* * *

At the Armand plantation, Adrien couldn't believe what he was hearing.

"I'm telling you, Mr. Armand, it was a big bear . . . pit bull frickin' thing. Bullets didn't stop it!" said the goon who'd escaped.

"I can't listen to any more of this crap. Let's feed the damn gators," said Adrien.

"Boss, please, I wouldn't make this stuff up."

"I believe him, dear," Veronique interjected. "In rare occasions, a perfect storm of dark and light energies can cause anomalous phenomena. I believe that is what has happened here. Remy was murdered on the grounds on his parents' graves. To him, it would have been a sanctum, a holy place. For his blood to be spilled there for nefarious means, the clash of opposing energies could have created a vortex of mystical forces that culminated in the manifestation of a rougarou for the purpose of retribution."

"Great," Adrien replied. "Now we gotta deal with a damn rougarou—a shapeshifter. How the hell do we kill it?"

"Typically, an entity of vengeance cannot be killed and only ceases to be after it has attained restitution," Veronique replied. "Seeing that those who carried out Remy's killing are deceased and the rougarou still exists, it stands to reason that restitution has not been attained. The disconcerting reality is that the target of its vengeance is . . . *you*, my love."

"Unbelievable," Adrien sighed. "You said *typically* it can't be killed. That means there is a way to kill it, right?"

"Yes," she replied. "A rougarou can be killed by another rougarou."

"Well, there you have it," Adrien responded, relieved. "Let's get us a rougarou and kill this asshole once and for all."

Veronique, not willing to outsource her mystical retribution, replied, "It's not that simple, my love. Most prospects do not survive the ritual to become a rougarou. It requires one mentally and physically strong enough to survive being bonded with the primal essence of the chosen animal spirit. If the candidate isn't up to the task, they will either die during the process or go mad, indiscriminately killing until being put down."

"I can do it," Antoine said with confidence. "I'm strong enough. Plus, I got a score to settle with Pittman."

"You sure you're up to this, baby bro?"

"I've always been as ornery as a gator."

* * *

Across town, a different type of ritual was taking place— one steeped in the symbiotic bond between mentor and student, father and son, both working toward a common goal.

"Calm," Coach said in a soothing tone as he observed Remy hitting the heavy bag. "Calm is the key—calm and controlled."

A master tactician in the sweet science, Coach had been contemplating ways to help Remy thrive and cope with his predicament since that night he returned as the Pit. The solution, Coach determined, was a simple one: utilize visualization to remain calm and controlled.

With visualization, Remy would mentally rehearse the actions he would perform, imagining the events unfolding in the way he desired them to. He imagined what he would feel, what he would see, what he would hear. Always, the goal was to assert control over the unbridled energies within him, focusing on a calm state of mind and fluidity in movement.

27

Whenever feelings of savagery would arise, he would focus his thoughts on his breathing, and the distracting thoughts would go away. Though the savage feelings were always accessible, these methods allowed him to control his urges and not let them control him.

Remy's power and speed were unfathomable—raw and unrefined. Coach believed that there were always things that a fighter could improve upon, and that thinking otherwise was the path to defeat. Unrivaled strength and speed might seem like the pinnacle to some, but Coach understood that great power could become a detriment when unchecked.

And with this philosophy in mind, Coach determined that the strategy to help Remy improve was that of less being more—less power, less speed, more control.

"Just take it easy," Coach reminded as Remy threw quick, thudding blows to the bag, restraining enough power to keep the bag intact. "That's it. Looking good. Control, Remy, that's the key. Be able to turn it off and turn it on. Time!"

Remy threw a final shot on the bag and let out a sigh of relief.

"Don't tell me you're winded," Coach exclaimed.

"No, it's not that," Remy replied. "It's weird. It takes conscious effort for me to restrain myself. My body feels fine, but it's taxing mentally."

"That's okay," said Coach. "That's the point. That's control. It doesn't have to be easy; it just has to be done."

Remy nodded in agreement.

"You ready?" Coach asked as he put on the punching mitts. "We been putting in the work to get back on the same page like we used to be. You can do it. *We* can do it."

"Let's work!" Remy said confidently, and they began.

The continuous pitter-patter of gloves on pads indicated that their hard work was paying off and that they were achieving the synchronized state that distinguished their mitt work. The pace quickened and the pops grew louder, and they both kept pace and didn't miss a beat. Though moving at a pace that most professionals couldn't maintain, Remy could tell that Coach was becoming winded, so he tapered his exertion to match his effort.

"Light work, light work," Coach would repeat as encouragement for himself and Remy.

The timer signaled that thirty seconds was left in the round. Remy decided to put their hard work to the test and closed his eyes.

The rapid pops continued, their rhythm unbroken as Remy forwent his sight and trusted in the bond he and Coach had developed through the years.

"That's it!" Coach said ecstatically. "Get it! Get it! Get it!"

The timer signaled the end of the round. "Time!" Coach yelled, and they embraced in celebration.

* * *

Human sacrifices were a common practice for the Armands, for the blood of rivals and associates alike was the fuel that powered their criminal empire. Typically, the dark rites called for human lives, but the *ritual of the rougarou* was different.

A misconception about the nature of the rougarou was that it regarded werewolves specifically, being a person with the ability to shapeshift into an anthropomorphic wolf. In reality, a rougarou could be in the form of any beast, typically predators with natural weapons that made them efficient killers. Wolves were common across the world, but rougarous often came in the form of habitat-specific beasts such as tigers, polar bears, and hyenas.

It seemed natural, almost inevitable, that Gator would choose to bond with the "king of the swamp."

The ritual would take place in the dark sanctum in the midst of the catacombs beneath the Armand plantation. The circular sanctuary was wide, with high stone walls lit with torches all around. Outside of the entrance stood four armed guards; only adepts were allowed inside.

A wide, circular altar stone rose in the middle of the sanctuary. Before it stood Veronique wearing her queenly vestments and holding a golden box. To her right was Adrien in ceremonial robes. To her left stood Antoine, wearing only sandals and a loincloth. Spaced evenly around the room stood six hooded acolytes in reverent silence.

Veronique handed the box to Adrien, who carefully opened it. Veronique took from it a bloody heart, freshly cut from the largest male alligator in their stock. She walked around the altar and rounded its edges with the heart, and then stepped upon it and drew a pentagram with its blood inside the circumference.

She stepped down and spoke to Antoine. "It's time."

Antoine nodded and stepped out of his sandals onto the altar. He lay inside the pentagram, his head at the southern vertex, his limbs at their corresponding vertices.

Antoine lay motionless as all in the room began repeating a chant in a language unknown to him; the only word he could pick out was rougarou.

The circle of blood suddenly ignited, and the blood making up the pentagram seemed to come alive and rose to cover every inch of Antoine's body. It was agonizing, like his whole body was on fire. He gritted his teeth in pain and emitted a low growl, but he refused to cry out. The blood seemed to absorb into his skin, and the fire dissipated.

His pupils turned to vertical slits, and his eyes became bloodshot. He stood as his muscles began to swell and his bones elongated. He let out a terrible cry that became a roar as thorn-like structures began to rise from his back, splitting away his alabaster skin to reveal dark-green, vertical columns of jagged scutes. His tailbone jutted and burst from his rear, growing longer and broader, dangling off the altar to the floor. His mouth widened in a fiendish smile as his gumline burst forth from his mouth into a long, rounded snout—splitting his lips as his human face peeled away.

His transformation complete, Antoine had truly become *the Gator*. Standing eight feet tall with a wide tail just as long, the Gator looked around at the spectators with sadistic intentions.

Unaware of their impending doom, the onlookers reveled in the transformation of their supposed champion. Little did they know that the ritual had actually failed. Indeed, Antoine was strong and determined enough to endure the physical agony of fusing with the primordial essence of the beast, but mentally he wasn't up to the task. To one with a weak mind, feelings of invincibility combined with savage urgings triggered a state of berserk rage, and the rational mind capitulated to the primal.

"Antoine, the ritual is complete. How do you feel?" Veronique asked, gazing smugly at the marvelous testament to her prowess as a voodoo queen.

Gator reached down and grabbed her, his massive webbed claw nearly encompassing her entire torso. He raised her to his gaping maw, chomped her head off, and tossed the spurting carcass to the side.

"What the hell!" Adrien shouted as he backed away in horror.

The terrified acolytes attempted to flee. Gator leapt from the altar, and with a single swipe of his tail, he cleaved three of them in two.

By that time, the four guards had realized that something had gone awry, and they rushed through the large double doors and took aim.

The Gator was stalking Adrien when he received a salvo of bullets. The remaining acolytes took the chance to escape.

Gator turned toward the gunmen and let out a roar so piercing that it ruptured their eardrums, causing two of them to fall to the floor, disoriented, clutching their ears. The Gator closed in, stomping one of their heads flat; the other he snatched up in his jaws and snapped in two.

The remaining gunmen regained their composure and continued to fire. The Gator lurched forward and dispatched one with an eviscerating downward swipe of its claw.

"Antoine!" Adrien yelled from behind him.

The Gator spun around, the swing of its tail splashing the last guard against the wall in a splatter of crimson mist.

Adrien stood before the beast, more dejected than afraid. "Baby bro, what the hell, man. Can you even understand me? I'm sorry, bro. I never wanted any of this crap for you. You were supposed to make it legit—make it big. This is all that Pittman's fault. I'm so sorry."

Even in his berserk state, one of his brother's last words struck a nerve: Pittman.

* * *

Back at Coach's, Remy and his mentor were saying what could possibly be their last goodbyes.

"Here, I want you to wear these." Coach presented Remy with a pair of black jogger shorts he'd had custom-fit for the Pit.

"They're stretchy," Coach chuckled, "so you won't have your ass out. Plus, check this out . . . a hole for your tail!"

Remy laughed. "Thanks, Coach."

"Remy, you're like a son to me. If things were different, there's no way I would let it go down like this. If it was just some get-back over some street beef, I mean. If that was the case, you let the law handle it. That's what I always told you, at least."

"Yes, sir," Remy responded humbly.

"But this ain't that. This ain't common. This don't even make common sense. What the hell are we supposed to say? 'Officer, I'd like to report a murder. Here's the victim.'

"I know one thing for sure, and that is, whatever set these events in motion is beyond our understanding. You feel that you have to go after them, and I support you. You've become someone more powerful than anything I've ever seen. Bullets don't faze you. You destroy anything you hit.

"And now, you can control it. You can change into the Pit at will. But remember, don't change your attitude: stay calm. When you're calm, you can think. When you're thinking, you'll make the right decisions. I'm at peace. I love you, son."

The two embraced, and Remy's dark eyes became a fiery amber.

* * *

The Pit's head rose from the murk of the Mississippi in front of the marina of the Armand plantation. Coach suggested that an aquatic approach would be the most clandestine. As he crept to shore, his senses alerted him that things were amiss. Something didn't smell right, literally—the scent of blood hovered in the air like a haze.

As he made his way through the woodlands and various quarters of the vast compound, he discovered why. It looked as though a battle had taken place—the grounds and structures were strewn with bodies and bullet holes. The corpses were dismembered and desecrated—the alligators common to the habitat taking advantage of the carrion.

"Pittman!" came a thundering roar from somewhere in the midst of the plantation. "I know you're here," the voice continued. "Your mangy stink betrays you!" it laughed. "I'll be waiting in the alligator pen."

Remy was dumbfounded. What was this thing? Whatever it was, it was clearly unnatural, its voice resonating like a loudspeaker.

Remy learned long ago to face fears head-on, but the unknown always presented anxiety.

Whatever it is, it picked the wrong one.

The thing taunted him as it guided him into its location. "You're getting closer, good boy," it laughed. "You don't know how long I've waited for this!"

The Pit looked up at the signage over the metal double doors: ALLIGATOR PEN. With a nonchalant kick, he blasted in the doors, obliterating a sizable chunk of the wall.

The Pit stepped through the dusty haze, snarling and ready to fight.

He had seen Gator's over-the-top training facility on TV before in all-access videos, but seeing it in person, it was both impressive and ridiculous at the same time. *This is what happens when you give stupid people lots of money.*

He looked with awe upon the Gator, standing with his arms crossed in the center of the ring.

"Remy Pittman!" the Gator said with glee. "I've been waiting for this day since you beat me at regionals. This time, we play for keeps!"

Remy couldn't believe what he was witnessing. The colossal monstrosity standing in the ring was really Antoine Armand. *How could this be?*

"Armand? You've changed."

"I have. It seems the blood of my enemies is the ultimate PED. Looks like I have the height and reach advantage now!"

"I never considered you to be an enemy," Pittman said. "We were rivals, but that's what we do. You tried to have *me* killed!"

"*All Pittman's fault*, my brother said. I was more than willing to see you in the ring. But things have been set in motion that cannot be undone. Adrien is dead, and now I am in charge. The spirit of the rougarou has chosen me to be the *King of the Swamp*. Sorry, but that means you have to die."

Pittman smirked. "You've grown a little, but you're still the same twerp."

The Gator let out a blaring roar and leapt from the ring onto the floor. He took hold of the ring and hoisted it above his head, its frame buckling and creaking. Pittman simply sidestepped as it crashed into the spot he'd previously been.

The two advanced toward each other. The Gator was quick for a hulking brute, but nowhere near as fast as Pittman. The invocation of the rougarou imparted the avatar with the strengths of the particular beast to excess—but often, mere physics was responsible for shortcomings. Though exceedingly powerful and enormous, alligators were not fashioned to be particularly efficient killers on land.

As the two converged, the Gator led with a hooking swipe with decapitating intentions.

Pittman ducked the blow and rolled outside of it and returned with a hook to the body. A backhand swing off the missed swipe caught the Pit at the same time on his high guard and sent him skidding. The Gator charged and led with a right straight, which the Pit also managed to duck, but the Gator stepped through and spun with the momentum into a tail swipe that caught the Pit in the gut and sent him crashing through the reinforced glass of the alligator tank.

The contents of the tank, alligators and all, spilled from the raised platform in a turbulent deluge. *Now I'm pissed.* The Pit, enraged and snarling, leapt from the tank to the floor below.

The Gator chortled.

"Lucky shot," Pittman snarled, and he charged full-bore at his foe.

In reality, it wasn't a lucky shot. Overconfident in his abilities, Remy seemed to have forgotten his recent lessons on remaining calm and instead opted to assert his dominance over his opponent with force—a bad idea when matched against such a daunting foe. Savagery was the Gator's game, and playing by his rules was a losing endeavor.

Pittman closed on the Gator and unleashed punishing, alternating hooks to his body. Damaging blows indeed, but this was more than a test of fisticuffs to the Gator, his mind completely given over to animal instincts. He stretched his gaping muzzle and bit down, completely engulfing the Pit's head down to his sternum. He lifted the Pit and trashed about, tossing the lacerated body into a nearby pool in a crimson splash.

"Just like I always thought!" the Gator laughed.

So this is how it ends. The primal rage that had been so boisterous before was nowhere to be felt—as if it were whimpering away like a scalded dog.

As he sank facedown, he was flooded with memories. *Mom . . . Dad . . . Coach.* In the darkness, Coach's words came quietly: *Calm, and keep calm. That's most important, if you're going to win. It's not easy to appear calm, but if you do, then you'll win. Calm is natural, remember that.*

With that, the Pit opened his eyes with renewed vigor.

"Feast, my brothers. Tear him apart," the Gator instructed the alligators in the enclosure with Remy. Animals aren't stupid, though, and they kept their distance.

The Pit's head emerged from the depths, stoically walking up the bank. The wounds in his chest were mending, but not as quickly as they would if inflicted by natural means.

"Nice work, Antoine," he said. "Ready for round two?"

Gator unleashed his powerful roar, but it merely ruffled the Pit's whiskers.

"You've always been a loudmouth," Pittman replied.

Incensed, Gator charged the Pit with a straight right. Remy ducked it and leapt over the ensuing tail swipe. Gator refocused on the Pit after completing his spin, and then lashed out with a lead-hand swipe, followed again by the tail. The Pit simply ducked the swipe and arched back to avoid the tail.

The Gator roared in anger and pressed the attack. Gator was crazed, attacking constantly, but to no avail. Pittman evaded every attack smoothly and countered with precision in a masterful display of defensive prowess. After some time, the Gator was exhausted, his supernatural stamina not as boundless as believed when taxed by unnatural means.

At the moment of truth, the two behemoths locked eyes, but their intentions couldn't have been more disparate: The Gator, ready to die; the Pit, ready to win.

The Gator initiated the charge, roaring as he shot forward. The Pit raced forward in kind.

As they closed, the Gator led with a jab, and the Pit slipped to the outside. Gator followed with a backhand strike with the same hand, and the Pit rolled under it to the inside, simultaneously loading up for a leaping lead uppercut.

Both knew the outcome before the actions had completed.

The blow smashed through the underside of the Gator's jaw and exploded out the top of his head.

The Pit withdrew his fist, tossing the Gator's carcass to the floor in the process.

He stood solemnly over his foe as the hulking Gator dissolved into Antoine's likeness, from the shoulders up, a crumpled hollow.

* * *

"And that's that," Coach finished, forthrightly.

At the conclusion of Coach's fantastic tale, CJ looked at him like he had to be joking. *This man has finally lost his mind.*

They looked squarely in each other's eyes, each waiting for the other to fold.

CJ broke first. "You know what, Coach, that's an incredible story you have there. You should submit it to a creative writing contest. You'll win because of the unique characters alone: a werepitbull, wereterrier, I guess, and weregators. *Okay.* Good stuff."

"CJ, look—" Coach started, before being interrupted.

"No, it's okay, Coach. Believe me, I understand. If I knew something about what happened to the people responsible for Remy's . . . well, I'd be tight-lipped too. Anyway, I gotta go, Coach. Paperwork, it never ends. It was good seeing you."

"Good seeing you too, CJ. So does the investigation continue?" he asked.

"That's where things get messy. Before we could even get forensics to the Armand estate, the Feds had swooped in and cordoned the place off, citing RICO. It's out of the NOPD's hands from here. I'm truly sorry, Coach. I'll do what I can about Remy's case, but things don't look too promising."

"I understand," said Coach. "Thank you, CJ. Take care now."

"You too, Coach," she replied, and then she went her way.

From the window, Coach watched her drive off as Remy walked up from behind.

"I could have shown her," Remy said. "I can control it, you know." Remy gave a showy grin as his dark eyes turned a fiery amber and his canines elongated.

"Cut it out. In due time," Coach replied. "Something she said got me concerned, so I think it's best we see how things play out."

"I was listening to everything y'all said, Coach. What are you so worried about?"

"I saw some weird things overseas, stuff that would be on the news if the government were honest. But in the Army, we just did our job and said those decisions were above our paygrade. What concerns me ... are the Feds."

* * *

At the Armand plantation, Federal forensics teams were busy at work, running to-and-fro, while specialized troops in black fatigues secured the perimeter in conjunction with the choppers above.

In the subterranean, dark sanctum in the midst of the catacombs, the officer-in-charge was on the phone with his superiors. "Yes, sir, from the looks of it, the dark sacrament was successful. I'm now standing in the hall where it was initiated. Those evil bastards finally got what was coming to them ... No, that's the mystery, sir. The zoanthrope appears to have decimated the Armand syndicate, but it was eliminated by another . . . It's unknown, sir. We know of no other zoanthropes in the vicinity, but it appears to be . . . on our side."

We'd like to know if you enjoyed the book. Please consider leaving a review on the platform from which you purchased the book

CPSIA information can be obtained
at www.ICGtesting.com
Printed in the USA
BVHW041350250523
664860BV00006B/174